Arab AMERICANS

SPIRIT
of America®

Arab AMERICANS

By C. Ann Fitterer

The Child's World®
Chanhassen, Minnesota

7

Arab AMERICANS

Published in the United States of America by The Child's World®
PO Box 326 • Chanhassen, MN 55317-0326 • 800-599-READ • www.childsworld.com

Acknowledgments
The Child's World®: Mary Berendes, Publishing Director

Editorial Directions, Inc.: E. Russell Primm, Emily Dolbear, Sarah E. De Capua, and Lucia Raatma,
Editors; Linda S. Koutris, Photo Selector; Image Select International, Photo Research; Red Line
Editorial and Pam Rosenberg, Fact Research; Tim Griffin/IndexServ, Indexer; Chad Rubel, Proofreader

Photos
Cover/frontispiece: A group of Syrian children in New York City, circa 1910

Cover photographs ©: Corbis; Catherine Karnow/Corbis

Interior photographs ©: AKG-Images, Berlin, 6; Corbis, 7, 8; AKG-Images, Berlin, 9; Corbis, 10, 11;
Corbis, 14, 15 top, 15 bottom; Jim Stokes, 17; Corbis, 18; Getty Images, 19 top; Corbis, 19 bottom;
Gamma, 20; Corbis, 21 top, 21 bottom; Gamma, 22, 23; Getty Images, 24, 25 top; Corbis, 25 bottom,
26 top; Getty Images, 26 bottom; Corbis, 27 top, 27 bottom, 28.

Registration
The Child's World®, Spirit of America®, and their associated logos are the sole property and
registered trademarks of The Child's World®, Inc.

Library of Congress Cataloging-in-Publication Data
Fitterer, C. Ann.
  Arab Americans / by C. Ann Fitterer.
      p. cm.
  Includes index.
  Summary: A simple overview of the heritage, customs, and beliefs of Arab
Americans.
  ISBN 1-56766-150-5 (library bound : alk. paper)
  1. Arab Americans—Juvenile literature. [1. Arab Americans.] I. Title.
  E184.A65 F58 2002
  973'.04927—dc21
                              2001007804

13   19   28

Contents

Chapter ONE

The First Arab Americans

A page from the Koran written in Arabic calligraphy

THE PEOPLE OF AMERICA CAN TRACE THEIR **ancestors** to countries throughout the world. For hundreds of years, people from other countries have left their homes to start a new life in America. Some groups have been in America for hundreds of years. Others have been in America for only a short time.

Arab Americans are a group of people who came to live in America during the last 150 years. Some arrived in the 1800s, and many others came in the 1900s. Arab **immigrants** are people who speak Arabic, the Arab language.

It is not always easy to identify the countries that the first Arab immigrants came from. It is difficult because Arab countries are located in an area known as the Middle East. This area is in southwestern

A wedding procession in Syria

Asia. Most of the countries lie east of the Mediterranean Sea. People in this area have been fighting one another for a long time. As they win and lose battles over land, the boundaries of the countries—and even the names of the countries—change.

The first Arab immigrants came from a place known as Mount Lebanon in a land called Syria. The people of Syria, called Syrians, heard of opportunities to make a lot of money in America. Some Syrians decided to move to America and live there for the rest of their lives. But most Syrians planned to work in America for just a few years and make a lot of money. They planned to save

Many Arab Americans plant a grapevine and a fig tree in their gardens. These plants represent their love of the land.

7

Some Arabs, such as this Syrian woman, followed the Christian religion.

this money and return to their homes and families in Syria. They would use the money they made in America to live a better life in Syria. Most of these people never returned to Syria, however. Most immigrants stayed in the United States.

The religion of these first Arab immigrants was Christianity. They were Christians. Some people in Arab countries followed the faith of Islam. These people were Muslims. They were not as likely to go to America because very few Muslims lived in America. The Arab Muslims were afraid that life would not be easy in a country where they were the only people of their faith.

In the 1900s, fighting between Arab people got worse. Christians were fighting Muslims. One group of Muslims was fighting another group of Muslims. Soon, Arabs were fighting people of the Jewish faith, too. More Arabs were coming to the United States to escape war. Not all the Arab immigrants were Christian. In recent years, many immigrants from Arab countries have been Muslim.

Between 1880 and 1914, 112,000 Arabs came to the United States. Then, in 1924, the U.S. government passed laws that limited the number of people who could move to the United States. Only 100 people per year could come to the United States from Arab countries. The governments of Arab countries had also been worried. They had watched their strongest and smartest young men and women leaving their countries. They were afraid that they would not have the right people to serve in the military and to take leadership positions in their governments. So the governments of Arab countries tried to stop Arabs from leaving their own countries.

A barricade marking the street during the Israel-Palestine conflict of 1948

After World War II (1939–1945), another wave of immigrants from Arab countries arrived in the United States. These immigrants

Many Palestinian families lost their homes in Israel.

were different from those who came earlier. These new immigrants were well-educated Muslims. Most of them came from an area called Palestine. Today, part of Palestine is known as the state of Israel. Israel is a **republic** that was founded in 1948 as a homeland for Jews. Many of the Muslims who had lived in this part of Palestine lost their homes at that time. Some moved to other Arab countries or to the United States. Others stayed to fight the Jews and regain their homeland.

Today, Muslims and Jews in many parts of the world continue to fight one another. Many Arab people come to America to escape the fighting in their homelands—the area we now call Israel. These people did not have a home. They could no longer live in Palestine. Their land had been given to another government and renamed Israel. Today, many Arab people still come to the United States to escape the fighting and war in their homeland.

ONE OF THE WORLD'S MAJOR religions is the faith of Islam. People who follow this religion are called Muslims. Islam is similar to Christianity and Judaism in that its followers believe in one god.

Almost 1,500 years ago, a boy named Muhammad was born in the city of Mecca (left), in what is now Saudi Arabia. As a man, Muhammad traveled and shared teachings and beliefs. The faith of Islam grew from his teachings.

The holy book of Islam is called the Koran. The teachings in this book are known as the Holy Law. Many governments in Arab countries are based on the Koran. The people live their daily lives according to the rules of the Holy Law. One rule is that they do not eat meat from pigs. Another rule makes Friday their day of worship.

Muslims follow the Five Pillars of Faith—which tell Muslims what they must do. For example, Muslims must visit the city of Mecca at least once in their lifetime. They must also observe the holy month known as Ramadan. During this time, Muslims **fast** during the daylight hours.

Hard Work and Success

THE ARAB IMMIGRANTS OF THE 1800S WERE not like the immigrants who came from European countries. Many European immigrants settled in the **rural** areas of America and farmed. Most of the other European immigrants worked in the factories of the bigger towns and cities.

The Arab immigrants were hard workers, but neither farming nor factories appealed to them. They were interested in trading. They liked selling things. This allowed them to work for themselves. They wanted to be their own bosses. They wanted to decide when to work and how hard to work.

These traders were called peddlers. They often carried a large box or trunk that was attached to a strong strap. The peddler

fastened this strap across his shoulders so that he could carry the box. In the box were many different objects to sell. The peddlers did not usually sell to people who lived in towns and cities. These people could buy the things they needed at stores.

The people who lived in the country could not easily get to a store when they needed things, though. So the peddlers packed their trunks with things they knew people living in the country might need. They traveled on foot

Many Syrians settled in New York City. They too were peddlers selling food and other things from street carts.

Interesting Fact

In the 1800s, the entire population of an Arab village came to America together with the hope of becoming rich.

13

or on horseback and stopped at each house.

Often, these peddlers were the only visitors the farm wives would have. They were happy to see the peddlers so they could buy what they needed.

Being a peddler was not an easy job, but the Arab immigrants were successful. Not only did they earn good money, but they quickly became part of the American **culture**.

The Arab immigrants knew that they needed to speak English to be truly successful. They worked hard to learn English. The time they spent visiting the homes of Americans helped them to learn English and to learn about the American way of life.

Many immigrants lived in a part of a town or city where other immigrants from the same country lived. These people could go home and speak their **native** language instead of speaking English. They lived in much the same way as they had lived in their home countries. This way of life often kept them from blending into the American way of life.

This was not true for the Arab immigrants, however. Because the peddlers were constantly

traveling, they were not able to live with people from their home countries. Also, they had to speak English most of the time. As a result, they were not isolated from the American way of life.

Many Arab immigrants saved the money they made as peddlers. Only a few Arab immigrants actually returned to their home-lands, though. Most used that money to open stores. They settled in towns and sent for their families to join them.

In the 1900s, Arab immigrants began working in factories. Working conditions in

Inside a Syrian food market on New York City's Washington Street in 1919

factories had improved by then and the workers were earning higher wages. These Arab Americans lived in cities, usually in neighborhoods where other Arab Americans lived.

By the 1920s, Arab Americans were living all across the United States. Although most of them worked in business, others worked in **manufacturing** and in education. They had become a part of the American culture.

A silk factory in Paterson, New Jersey, where a large number of workers were Arab American

W̲HEN NEW IMMIGRANTS STARTED TO WORK AS PEDDLERS, THEY gathered together in peddler settlements. After being on the road, the peddlers would return to their peddler settlement. There they would eat, drink, sing, and talk with other

peddlers. This way of life reminded the peddlers of the villages in their home countries and helped them to deal with homesickness. They were able to talk in Arabic, their native language.

Usually, many peddlers lived together in small and dark rooms. Often, the rooms had neither heat nor furniture. Although the peddlers had the money to live in better homes, they wanted to save their money rather than spend it on housing. Some peddlers used the money they earned to buy a horse cart, or later, even a car.

Traveling as a peddler could be dangerous, so peddlers often traveled together. Those who traveled on foot had a hard job. Their packs weighed up to 200 pounds (91 kilograms)!

Chapter THREE

Arab-American Life

IN THEIR DETERMINATION TO BE SUCCESSFUL IN America and follow the American way of life, Arab Americans lost many of the **traditions** of their own culture. Because they were scattered across the country, there were few neighborhoods where people spoke Arab languages or practiced Arab traditions.

In the early 1900s, Arab-American children knew little of Arabic traditions.

Some things, though, did not change for the Arab people when they moved to America. In their homelands, Arabs were known for being hard workers. This quality helped them **adapt** to the

American culture.
In America, Arab
immigrants and
their Arab-American
children work hard.
    Arab people
have always
believed in the
value of a good

education. Some immigrants came to
America to get a better education than they
could have received in their homelands.

Arab Americans highly value a good education.

    Family has always been important in the
Arab culture. As Arab families came to join

The family unit remains important to Arab Americans.

19

their relatives in America, they lived together. The Arab immigrants were good citizens. They were careful to follow American laws and to act **responsibly**.

Arab immigrants who came to the United States during the past 50 years also share these values of work, education, and family. But there is a difference between them and the Arabs who came to America before the 1950s. These newer immigrants do not feel a need to become "Americanized" as quickly as the early Arab-American peddlers and businessmen did.

Today, some Arab Americans wear traditional dress even while shopping in modern American stores.

Most recent Arab Americans are Muslim. They have settled together in American towns and cities. They have found places to worship together, and their faith keeps them focused on their native cultures. These things can also make it difficult for them to fit into the American way of life, however.

Several obstacles make it hard for Arab immigrants to fit easily into American society. To begin with, they do not speak English.

Also, their clothes are different. And the rules and traditions of their Muslim faith are unfamiliar to many Americans.

Over the past several decades, Arab Americans have become more interested in learning about Arab traditions. Many of them are learning to speak Arabic. Places of worship, called mosques, have been built in many American cities, and many Arab Americans have traveled to their homelands. Many still have family members and relatives living there.

Mosques (above in Los Angeles and below in Washington, D.C.) can be found throughout the United States

Many organizations focus on Arab culture today, and some help people keep Arab traditions. Others help Arabs get good educations and jobs. Some organizations help Arab immigrants adjust to life in America, or they work to help different groups of people understand one another better.

21

AN IMPORTANT TIME OF YEAR FOR MUSLIM PEOPLE IS A MONTH IN THE Islamic calendar called Ramadan. The Islamic calendar is based on the cycles of the moon. The 12-month Western calendar is based on the cycles of the sun. One of the 11 months of the lunar calendar is Ramadan. It is either 29 or 30 days long, depending on the year.

During Ramadan, Islamic people fast. A person who is fasting does not eat or drink. Every healthy Muslim adult must fast during

Ramadan. They do it as an important part of their devotion to God. Fasting allows people to understand what a poor person experiences. It helps them understand why they must help the poor and work to make their lives better. It also helps them develop self-control. It is hard not to eat or drink when you are hungry or thirsty.

Fasting during Ramadan does not mean that one cannot eat anything, though. Actually, the fasting begins each day at sunrise and lasts until sunset. In the evening after the sun has set, a light meal is eaten. Traditional Ramadan pancakes are called *kattaif* (above).

The night between the 26th and the 27th days of Ramadan is called the Night of Determination. According to the Koran, God determines the course of world events for the coming year on this night.

The day after Ramadan is called Fast-Breaking (opposite). Muslims celebrate this day with special prayers and festivals.

Chapter *Four*

Arab-American Contributions

A patriotic bumper sticker in a predominantly Arab neighborhood in Dearborn, Michigan

ALTHOUGH ARAB AMERICANS HAVE been an important part of American culture for almost 150 years, they still struggle to be accepted by all Americans. Sometimes they experience **prejudice**.

For several reasons, life can be difficult today for some Arab Americans. The U.S. government has become involved with the governments of several Arab countries. The U.S. government has also helped Israel. And America has fought against some Arab countries in wars. All these things have angered many Arab people in the United States, and they have spoken out against America.

Some people in Arab countries commit acts of **terrorism**. Terrorist activities kill innocent people and cause fear in others. Terrorists try to scare people into doing what the terrorists want. Many Americans blame acts of terrorism on all Arabs instead of just those individuals who were involved. Arab Americans often remind people that not all Arabs act like the few who are terrorists.

Ralph Nader has worked for years to protect American consumers.

Today, Arab Americans are a part of every aspect of American culture. Some of the country's most important educators, business-people, and government leaders have been Arab American. Edward Said, a distinguished professor of literature at Columbia University in New York City, is one such scholar. Ralph Nader is a famous Arab-American lawyer. He has worked hard to pass laws that make life better and safer for all Americans. In 2000, Nader ran for president of the United States.

Najeeb Halaby, pilot and former head of Pan American Airways

Najeeb Halaby is a lawyer, test pilot, former head of Pan American Airways, adviser to three U.S. presidents, and former

Kahlil Gibran, *author of* The Prophet

head of the Federal Aviation Administration. He is also the father of a queen! His daughter, Lisa Halaby, married King Hussein of Jordan in 1978 and became Queen Noor.

Arab Americans are active in the literary arts as well. An early Arab-American immigrant was Kahlil Gibran. His book *The Prophet*, published in 1923, has sold more than 8 million copies. Gibran was also an accomplished painter. William Peter Blatty wrote a humorous story about growing up as an Arab American called *Which Way to Mecca, Jack?* He is more famous for having written the novel *The Exorcist*. St. Louis-born Naomi Shihab Nye is one of the most famous Arab-American poets. She also writes children's books and novels for young adults.

Heisman Trophy–winner Doug Flutie

Arab Americans have also made contributions as athletes. Doug Flutie is an NFL quarterback. In 1984, Flutie became the first college quarterback to win the Heisman Trophy in 13 years. The Heisman Trophy is awarded each year to the best college football player in the United States.

Casey Kasem is an Arab American who has become famous in entertainment. Millions of radio listener's recognize his famous voice. Kasem is the host of "American Top 40," playing the top 40 songs in the country each week. He is equally as famous to cartoon fans as the voice of Shaggy in the Scooby-Doo television series as well as some films. Paula Abdul's records have sold millions of copies around the world. Before she became famous as a singer, she worked as a dancer and **choreographer**. Paul Anka is a well-known singer and songwriter. Frank Zappa was a brilliant rock guitarist, film director, and orchestral composer. Jamie Farr, Kathy Najimy, Tony Shalhoub, Danny Thomas, and Marlo Thomas are all famous Arab-American actors.

Singer, dancer, and choreographer Paula Abdul

Arab foods, such as pita bread, hummus, and babba ghannouj, are popular in the United States.

Many people in the United States enjoy Arab-American food. Appetizers such as *hummus* and *babba ghannouj* are popular appetizers. Hummus is a dip made from crushed chickpeas, and babba ghannouj is a dip made from eggplant. *Falafel* is also cooked using crushed chickpeas, but the batter is

Interesting Fact

▸ Detroit, Michigan, and Paterson, New Jersey, have the largest Arab-American populations.

Many Arab Americans are proud of their patriotism.

rolled into little balls that are then fried to make a crunchy treat. Several dishes include lamb, chicken, and beef and are served with warm pita bread or rice. Pita bread is usually round in shape, flat, and can open up like a pocket. *Couscous* is served as either a side dish or the main part of a meal. It is made from wheat kernels and has a texture that is very similar to rice. Hot sauce usually accompanies couscous. Desserts often contain dried fruits or nuts. Sometimes restaurants have a grocery store next door where people can buy ingredients to cook their own Arab-American food at home.

The United States clearly owes much to its millions of Arab-American citizens. Their courage, hard work, family values, and commitment to education strengthen and **enrich** the American way of life.

28

Time LINE

221 B.C   1848   2000s

1000 B.C Arabs are first mentioned in ancient records.

600 Islam, the religion of most Arabs, is founded by the prophet Muhammad

1492 Some historians believe this is the year when the first Arabs set foot on American soil, after departing from Moorish Spain with Columbus on his famous voyage.

1775–1783 Revolutionary War is fought and eventually won.

1876 Arabs participate in Philadelphia's Centennial Exposition.

1880–1914 More than 100,000 Arabs emigrate to the United States.

1890s Arab women begin emigrating to the United States.

1913 Arab-American author Kahlil Gibran forms the Pen League to encourage the Arab literary movement in the United States.

1920s Arab Americans are found throughout the United States.

1924 The U.S. government passes laws that limit immigration.

1939–1945 World War II is fought.

1948 Israel declares itself a state, and the resulting political conflicts cause many people from the region to move to the United States.

1953 Arab-American Danny Thomas gets his own television show called *Make Room for Daddy*.

1967 Israel defeats Egypt, Syria, and Jordan in the Six-Day War, causing residents in those regions to move to the United States in larger numbers.

1980 The American Arab Anti-Discrimination Committee is founded. Its aim is to influence American attitudes and government decisions about Arabs and the Middle East.

1984 Arab-American Doug Flutie wins the Heisman Trophy.

2000 Arab-American Ralph Nader runs for president of the United States.

2001 After the September 11 attack on the World Trade Center, Arab Americans face increased discrimination and misunderstanding.

2002 Approximately 3 million Arab-Americans live in the United States of America.

29

adapt (uh-DAPT)
To adapt is to change in a way that fits the surroundings. Arab Americans adapted well to life in the United States.

ancestors (AN-sess-turs)
Ancestors are family members, such as grandparents, and so on, who lived long ago. Americans trace their ancestors to countries all over the world.

choreographer (kor-ee-OG-ruh-fur)
A choreographer is someone who creates the steps to a dance. Paula Abdul is a well-known singer and choreographer.

culture (KUHL-chur)
A culture is a way of life, including ideas and traditions, shared by a group. Arabs have become part of the American culture.

enrich (en-RICH)
To enrich is to improve the quality of something. Arab Americans have enriched life in the United States in many ways.

fast (FAST)
To fast is to stop eating for a given period of time. Muslims fast during Ramadan.

immigrants (IM-uh-gruhnts)
Immigrants are people from one country that move to another country to live. Arab immigrants quickly learned English when they arrived in America.

manufacturing (man-yuh-FAK-chur-ing)
Manufacturing is the production of objects, usually by using machines. Some Arab Americans settled in cities and worked in manufacturing.

native (NAY-tiv)
Something that is native belongs to a person because of where he or she was born. Many European immigrants continued to speak their native languages, but Arab Americans were quick to learn English.

prejudice (PREJ-uh-diss)
Prejudice is an unfair opinion or treatment of a person based on his or her race, religion, or background. Many Arab Americans have faced prejudice.

republic (ri-PUHB-lik)
A republic is a type of government in which people elect their representatives. Israel is a republic founded in 1948.

responsibly (ri-SPON-suh-blee)
To act responsibly is to be sensible and trustworthy. Arab Americans have tried to follow U.S. laws and behave responsibly.

rural (RUR-uhl)
A rural area is one that is related to farming or located in the countryside. Many European immigrants settled in rural areas of the United States, while Arab immigrants chose the cities.

terrorism (TER-ur-ism)
Terrorism is the act of using violence and threats to frighten people. Some people in Arab countries commit acts of terrorism.

traditions (truh-DISH-uhns)
Traditions are customs, beliefs, and ideas handed down from one generation to another. Some Arab Americans have lost the traditions of their Arab culture, while others have rediscovered them.

For Further INFORMATION

Internet Sites

Visit our homepage for lots of links about Arab Americans:
http://www.childsworld.com/links.html

Note to Parents, Teachers, and Librarians:
We routinely verify our Web links to make sure they're safe,
active sites—so encourage your readers to check them out!

Books

Ameri, Anan, and Dawn Ramey, eds. *Arab American Encyclopedia.* Chicago: UoXoL®, 1999.

Ganeri, Anita. *I Remember Palestine.* Austin, Tex.: Raintree/Steck-Vaughn, 1995.

Hall, Loretta and Bridget K. *Arab American Biography.* Chicago: UoXoL®, 1999.

Harris, Nathaniel. *Israel and the Arab Nations in Conflict.* Austin, Tex.: Raintree/Steck-Vaughn, 1999.

Isaac, John (photographer), and Keith Elliot Greenberg. *The Middle East: Struggle for a Homeland.* San Diego: Blackbirch Press, 1996.

Long, Cathryn J. *The Middle East in Search of Peace.* Brookfield, Conn.: Millbrook Press, 1996.

Naff, Alixa. *The Arab Americans.* New York: Chelsea House Publishing, 1998.

Places to Visit or Contact

The American-Arab Anti-Discrimination Committee
4201 Connecticut Avenue, NW
Suite 300
Washington, D.C. 20008
202-244-2990

The Arab-American Cultural & Community Center
10555 Stancliff Road
Houston, TX 77099
713-783-2727

Arab American Institute
1600 K Street, N.W., Suite 601
Washington, DC 20006
202-429-9214

Index